Hasan
The Intelligent

A Series Of
Ancient Iraqi Tales
For Children

Book Name: Hasan, The Intelligent
Written by: Shafiq Mahdi, Misdaq R Syed
Edited by: Misdaq R Syed
Illustrated by: Tayyeba Tawassuli
Publisher: Al-Buragh for Children`s Culture
Design and technical supervision: Mohammed Alqasemi
Published Year: 2023
ISBN: 9789922704296

Hasan
The Intelligent

Written by: Shafiq Mahdi, Misdaq R Syed
Illustrated by: Tayyeba Tawassuli

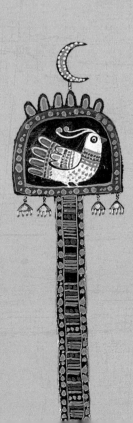

A long time ago, there lived a boy in one of the cities of Iraq. His name was Hasan. Hasan was an orphan. He had no parents or family to take care of him. He was homeless and had no job. Whenever he got hungry, he would go near food stands and eat the remains of what people had thrown. In this city, there lived a ruler who had three beautiful daughters. He was a very proud person who never considered the opinions of others. One day, the ruler decided to test his daughters. He ordered the daughters to be brought to him one by one.

First, the eldest entered and gave her greetings. The ruler posed a question to his eldest daughter, "Let me see, my daughter, is wisdom and intellect more important in life or wealth and power?" The eldest daughter answered, "Of course, wealth and power, dear father."

The ruler was pleased with the answer and gave the girl an expensive gift.

Then it was the middle one's turn. The ruler asked her the same question. The middle one answered the same. The ruler became happy again and she too, received an expensive gift.

6

Now it was the last girl's turn. The ruler asked her, "My dear daughter, what is the most important thing in life? Wealth and power, or intellect?"

The little girl thought and said, "Well of course, intellect are more important, dear father."

The ruler became upset by her answer. He said to her, "I shall make you understand the truth of what you have said." Then he called his minister and said, "Go find the most miserable and poor person in the city for me."

The minister looked for the poorest, most miserable person all over the city and finally found him. Yes, it was Hasan.

The minister took Hasan to the ruler and said, "My lord, this boy has nothing, not even food to eat."

The king wanted to teach his little daughter the truth of the matter. So he got her married to Hasan and bid them farewell. "Now go and live as you please, for you don't value wealth and power." The girl left with Hasan with the little money she had and a few pairs of clothes.

Hasan was dumbfounded. He could not believe that he just became the son-in-law of the ruler of the city. When the two of them left the palace, the ruler's daughter said, "Well, Hasan darling, where is your house that we may go to?"

Hassan said, "Uhhh … I don't have a house."

The girl asked in surprise, "Really? So, where do you sleep at night?"

Embarrassed as his face blushed, he couldn't answer her. "Don't be shy. I am your wife now; be at ease with me." She consoled him.

Hasan told her he sleeps on a bench near the park. The girl smiled when she saw Hasan's sleeping place. She gave him a coin she had and said, "Come, take this and sell it. Buy food and a knitting kit and some yarn with his money."

Then she gave him another coin to buy a rug so they have a place to sleep on.

Hasan went to the market with great embarrassment. After searching for a long time, he finally bought the things his wife had asked for.

That day, after eating and resting, Hasan's wife went and started knitting. She was quite handy with knitting. She knitted a beautiful shawl. She gave Hasan the address of a buyer and told him to take the shawl and sell it to him.

Hasan sold the shawl for two coins. He bought fruits with one coin and more yarn with the other.

The third day passed in the same manner. On the fourth day, his wife said, "Look, Hasan, you have to work too. I can't work while you sit idle."

The next morning, Hasan went to work and found work in construction. He worked tirelessly that day and in the evening received his first salary and was walking happily back to the park. On the way, he saw a strange man who had a cart while shouting, "I sell intellect! Come and buy intellect from me! Great offer!"

Hasan said to himself in surprise, "Is it even possible to buy intellect? Perhaps, there is truth to this matter. I shall surely benefit with intellect."

Hasan went to the man. He gave him all the money he had earned and asked him for intellect. The man searched inside his cart until he found it and said, "Listen carefully! And never forget! The intellect is contained in this phrase: Beauty is in the eye of the beholder!"

The man said this and walked away. Hasan regretted immediately, for he had lost his hard-earned money while seemingly not gaining anything. He went to the park and told his wife the story. His wife said with a smile, "The money you paid for this lesson is small. Tomorrow after your work, you'll make more money again so don't worry. Now go wash up while I prepare the meal."

The next day, Hasan went to work with hope and excitement.

Both husband and wife worked hard for several years and accumulated enough savings to buy a small piece of land where they built a small home for themselves. It wasn't anything fancy but it was better than sleeping in the park.

One day, the wife remarked to Hasan, "Thank God, with a lot of effort, our situation is better than before. What do you think about starting a business? Go to the market and see what the traders are buying and selling. Learn the art of business and work like them."

Hasan went to the market and started learning about the trading business. He heard that a large caravan was heading to Baghdad and would need necessary supplies for the trip. Hasan informed his wife and decided to go along with the caravan.

He bought a lot of goods and joined the caravan. They traveled far in the countryside until they reached a desert, which was devoid of any water and greenery; where there was no sign of life. They reached a well that had water but was very deep and hard to reach. Anyone that went deep inside the well did not come out. No one then dared to go into the well. They were dying of thirst, as were the camels.

Hasan decided to go down the well as he felt it was his duty to quench the thirst of his fellow travelers. But his companions advised against it as he was young and had just married. Hasan said, "Don't worry friends, I will go inside the well and fetch water." He asked God for help and put his trust in Him. He descended into the well slowly and carefully, one foot at a time until he almost reached the floor of the well when something grabbed hold of his right foot. It was a big, ugly genie that had been living there for thousands of years.

23

Next to the genie were two girls; one was very ugly and the other very pretty. The genie looked at Hasan with an intense glare and said, "Listen to me carefully, boy! Anyone who dared come here did not leave unless he answered my question correctly. Which of these two daughters of mine are more beautiful? Answer wrong and I will do what I did to the people before you."

Hasan thought anxiously. "Answer quickly! You seem to be as foolish as those before you," shouted the genie angrily.

Then Hasan remembered the phrase from that strange man who sold him intellect. He knew there was something tricky about the question as daughters are equally beautiful to the father. He told the genie, "Beauty is in the eye of the beholder."

The genie went into deep thought. Then looked at Hasan with excitement and exclaimed, "I have finally lost and you have won! Now ask me whatever you want, and you shall have it!"

Hasan asked for water for his companions. The genie fetched him some clean, refreshing water. Then he took Hasan to a room filled with gold and gems. "Take whatever you like, this too is your reward. But I fear your companions may conspire against you, so smear them with mud so that they think of it as worthless."

Hasan did what the genie advised and came out of the well with water and gold and gems covered in dirt. He watered his companions and the animals, then he loaded the gold and gems on his camel and continued his journey.

When he returned home, he recounted the story to his wife. "The intellect that I bought from the strange man really paid off! With all this wealth, we can buy a huge palace!"

His wife jokingly said, "You get a palace because of your intellect while I lost the palace because of mine!"

The couple bought a large piece of land in front of the ruler's palace and built a grander, more beautiful palace than it. When the ruler saw the palace in front of his palace, he wondered to himself, "Who could be the owner of this palace? Where did they get all this money to build such a magnificent palace?"

Hasan organized an opening ceremony and invited his friends and neighbors - including the ruler to his palace. Everyone was speechless when they entered the palace, for it was truly a magnificent, spectacular creation.

When it was time to eat, they brought food with fine, golden crockery and cutlery. Such delicious food that even the ruler hadn't tasted. When the ruler saw these things, he could not wait any longer. He had to ask. "Tell me about yourself. From where did you gather such wealth? You look much too young to have accumulated such wealth with work and effort." He inquired.

The ruler's daughter stood in front of him and said, "Do you not recognize us, Father? This man is Hasan, the same one who was the poorest in our city, lonely and orphaned. I am your daughter whom you kicked out of your palace. Do you see how intellect wins over wealth and power?"

The ruler was embarrassed by his shallow thinking and asked for forgiveness. He admitted to his mistake and invited Hasan to be a minister and a close advisor. Hasan had used his intellect, which gained the respect and admiration of the ruler and the people around him.

Made in the USA
Columbia, SC
03 May 2024

35063717R00022